A Purnell book
ISBN 0 361 03488 1
First published 1976. Reprinted 1987
Copyright © 1976 Express Newspapers plc
Printed by Purnell Book Production Ltd
Paulton, Bristol. A member of BPCC plc
Macdonald & Co (Publishers) Ltd
Greater London House, Hampstead Road
London NW1 7QX. A BPCC plc company

RUPERT
and the Mystery Voice

Illustrated by Bestall
Based on his original story

Purnell

CHAPTER 1

One bright sunny day, Rupert went out for a walk on the Common.

"I wonder if any of my pals will be out this morning," he thought to himself. "It would be nice to have someone to play with."

Just then he noticed Algy Pug walking along in front of him. He was quite a long way off, and it seeemed to Rupert as if Algy was wearing a policeman's helmet.

"I wonder what Algy's doing" thought Rupert. "Perhaps he's pretending to be a detective in search of clues! I'll sneak up behind him and give him a surprise!"

Tiptoeing through the bushes, Rupert soon caught up with Algy.

"Boo!" he said, loudly.

Algy turned round quickly and the thing on his head fell to the ground.

"Oh, Rupert, you did give me a shock!" he said. "Where did you spring from?"

"I saw you with that policemans's helmet on your head and thought you were playing detectives," said Rupert. "I say, what *is* that thing? It's not a helmet after all!"

"No, but I haven't the faintest idea what it is," said Algy, picking the bell-shaped object up. "I found it in the woods just now—

in fact, I stubbed my toe on it. People shouldn't leave litter lying around where people like me can stub their toes on things," he went on, "so I picked it up."

"It's black, and shiny, and it looks like a bell," said Rupert, "but it hasn't got a clapper inside it and it looks as if it screws into something. I've never seen anything like it before!"

The two pals were looking at the strange object so carefully that neither of them noticed a small figure creeping up behind them. Suddenly a hand reached out and grabbed the object from Algy's hand.

Before the friends had time to say a word the little person had run away.

"Well!" said Algy. "Who was that?"

Rupert ran to the top of the hill and looked across the Common at the little figure, speeding away.

"It's the Professor's servant!" he shouted to Algy. "We'll never catch him up now. I wonder why that funny object was so important to him?"

"Oh, never mind," said Algy, who had walked up to join him. "It wasn't any use to us, anyway. Who wants a funny old black bell that doesn't ring?"

"A bell, you say?" said a voice behind them.

Algy and Rupert turned to see the Professor himself standing behind them. "Have you two seen a black bell? Did it have a screw thing at one end?"

"Why yes, it did," admitted Algy. "Was it yours? I found it in the wood, and now your servant has taken it away."

"Good, good!" beamed the old Professor. Rupert opened his mouth to ask some questions about it, but the Professor turned on his heel and strode off down the hill after his servant.

"Well, really!" said Algy. "I wish someone would tell me what's going on! Come on, let's forget all about it and find something else to do."

"No, I'm interested!" said Rupert. "Let's follow them and see if we can discover anything."

So Algy and Rupert ran down the hill after the Professor. But at the bottom they met Mrs Bear.

"Oh, Rupert, I've been looking for you!" she said. "Constable Growler has told me that there is a dangerous thief on the loose and I've been worried that you might bump into him. Now come along home with me and play in the garden!"

"Oh dear, Mummy," sighed Rupert. "Have I got to?"

"Yes, you must," said Mrs Bear. "At least for this morning. He may have been caught by this afternoon, and you can go out to play then. Algy can come home with you if he likes."

CHAPTER 2

So Rupert and Algy went back to Rupert's cottage and played with Rupert's train set for the rest of the morning. Then Algy went home for his lunch.

"May I go out to play now, Mummy?" said Rupert, when he had eaten his meal.

"Well, all right, if you don't stray too far," said Mummy. But just then there was a knock at the door. Mrs Bear went to answer it, and there stood the Professor's servant.

"I have a message for Rupert from my master," said the servant. "He would like to know if Rupert would be kind enough to help him with an experiment."

Rupert jumped up from the table.

"Oh, I'd love to!" he cried. So he and the

Professor's servant set out across the Common.

"That was a funny thing you did this morning," said Rupert, as they walked along. "Why did you run away like that?"

Without answering Rupert's question, the servant suddenly ran away again!

"What a strange person!" thought Rupert. "He's always running off! I suppose I'd better follow him!"

But the servant had disappeared into the bushes and Rupert couldn't see him anywhere.

"I suppose he's headed into the wood," thought the little bear.

Just then Rupert heard a voice from the wood.

"Help! Help!" it called.

"Oh, someone is in trouble—I'll have to go

and see what's the matter!" thought Rupert. He started off into the wood, and had not gone far when he heard the voice again.

"Rupert!" it called.

"This time it sounds as if it's coming from behind me!" thought the puzzled little bear. So he retraced his footsteps to the edge of the wood again.

"Rupert!" came the voice, from above his head.

"That sounds like the Professor, but what is he doing up that tree?" thought Rupert,

as he looked up. "Well, there's only one thing for it—I'll have to climb the tree to find out!"

So up the tree went Rupert. He liked climbing trees and it wasn't too difficult to get to the top.

"Now where can he be?" thought Rupert.

There was no sign of anyone else in the branches, but, some distance away, he caught sight of his friends, Algy, Podgy and Willie.

"I'll climb down and ask them if they know what's going on!" decided Rupert. Scrambling down the tree as fast as he could go, he called to them.

"Why, Rupert, what *have* you been doing?" squeaked Willie. "You look as if you've been dragged through a hedge backwards!"

"I haven't, but I *have* been to the top of that high tree and down again!" said Rupert.

"I've been looking for the Professor. I heard his voice calling me for help but I can't find him anywhere!"

"Hello, hello, what's all this then?" said Constable Growler, who had come along the path just then.

"Oh, Constable Growler, how glad I am to see you!" said Rupert. "I've lost the Professor. He called to me from that tree over there, but he's not at the top of it so he must have slid down into the trunk and got locked in!"

"Hmm! Never heard of a tree capturing professors before," said Constable Growler, doubtfully. "Still, there's a first time for everything, I suppose, young bear."

With Rupert and his friends close behind him, he marched up to the tree.

"Come on out now, Professor, you've had your little game," he growled.

Nothing happened.

"Open up in the name of the law!" shouted Constable Growler.

Still nothing happened.

Constable Growler turned to Rupert.

"I've had enough of this," he said. "You're making fun of me. If the Professor was in that tree he'd have said something by now." He turned to the tree. "Sorry about that, tree," he said to the tree trunk. Then he walked away.

When Constable Growler was nearly out of sight, the tree spoke again. "Sorry about

that, Rupert," it said, in the Professor's voice, "but my servant is coming back to make everything right!"

Sure enough, the servant popped up out of a clump of bushes nearby. He was laughing so much that tears were running down his face.

"Come with me, little bear," he said "This time I promise I won't run away! You others stay here."

Amazed, Rupert followed him up the path. And there, sitting behind another tree, was the Professor!

"There you are!" exclaimed Rupert. "Am I glad to see you!"

"Thank you for helping me with my experiment, Rupert," laughed the Professor.

"You've been a very good assistant!"

"But I haven't done anything yet!" said Rupert. "And please tell me how you got up that tree and down again without me seeing you!"

The Professor reached behind him and brought out a strange wooden box. On the front was the bell-shaped object that Algy had found that morning, and a funny sort of black funnel on the top.

"I'm too old to climb trees, my young friend," said the Professor. "But I've learned to throw my voice through this amazing new invention of mine. I made it out of an old gramophone. I've got a new stereo system at home now to play my records on, so I've turned my old gramophone into a machine that makes my voice seem to come from all sorts of places. I can't tell you how it works because it's very difficult to explain, but when I twiddle these knobs I can direct my voice wherever I like!"

"Oh, how interesting!" cried Rupert. "Can I have a go, please?"

"Certainly," said the Professor. So Rupert spoke into the litttle funnel at the top of the machine, and the Professor turned the knobs.

It sounded just as if Rupert was speaking from the bushes several yards away!

"Do you know, you could use this machine as a sort of one-way telephone!" cried Rupert. "If I went into the woods, where you can't hear me if I shout, and projected my voice to where you're sitting, you'd be able to hear me quite clearly. Can I try it?"

"Yes, that's a good idea," agreed the Professor. So Rupert carried the machine deep into the woods.

"Here's a good spot to set up the machine,"

thought Rupert, as he came to an open patch of woodland. "Now—which way do I twiddle the knob to make my voice reach the Professor?"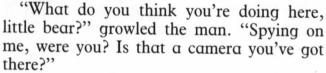

Suddenly a large hand gripped Rupert's shoulder, and he turned in fright to see who it was. A big, cross-looking man stood there.

"What do you think you're doing here, little bear?" growled the man. "Spying on me, were you? Is that a camera you've got there?"

"No—honestly it isn't!" said Rupert, who was very frightened.

"It's a tape recorder, then, is it?" snarled the man.

"No—it's . . . it's not a tape recorder!" gasped Rupert.

"Then it's a radio set!" said the man. "And you can't be up to any good in the wood with a radio set! You'd better come with me!" And he picked up the Professor's machine in one hand, and Rupert in the other.

"Oh dear, what am I going to do now?"

thought Rupert, as the man ran through the woods with him under one arm. "This must be the dangerous thief that Mummy told me about this morning! How I wish I'd stayed at home and never got mixed up with such a horrible man! And I do wish he would put me down. I'm feeling quite sick from being jolted about like this!"

Through the wood ran the man, jolting Rupert even more as he tripped over the twigs

and branches that were strewn on the ground.

"I do hope he doesn't drop the Professor's invention," thought Rupert, anxiously. "There isn't another one like it in the whole world, and he's spent such a lot of time getting it working properly."

CHAPTER 3

At last the man stopped running and put Rupert down outside a wooden hut deep in the woods.

"Get in there!" he said, opening the door and shoving the little bear inside.

It was very dark in the shed, and it took Rupert several minutes to peer through the gloom and get used to the darkness. Then he noticed that the man was sitting near him with the Professor's invention on his knee.

"I've never seen a radio set like this before," said the man. "It must be very valuable. How does it work?"

"Put it down!" said Rupert, boldly. "You might break it! It doesn't belong to you!"

"Ho! Ho!" laughed the man, in a horrible sort of way. "But taking things that don't belong to me is my business!"

"Oh!" gasped Rupert. "You must be the thief that Constable Growler is looking for!"

"They're all looking for me, but I'm too smart for them!" said the thief. "Now, are you going to show me how this works, or am I going to find out for myself?"

Rupert said nothing. He knew that if the thief realised what an unusual instrument it was, he would be even more keen to keep it for himself.

"That's it!" said the thief, turning a knob at the front. But, as he turned the knob, the machine threw his voice so that it sounded as if it was coming from outside the shed.

"Oh!" said the thief. "There's s-s-someone there!" Still it sounded as if the voice was coming from outside.

Getting up in fright, the thief ran to the door. He threw it open and dashed out to see who was there, not realising that it was his own voice that he had heard.

"Now's my chance!" thought Rupert. "I must try to escape before he returns!"

Quietly getting up from the floor of the shed, he ran to the door. But the thief had locked the door behind him.

"Oh dear, I'm locked in!" sighed Rupert. Then he glanced upwards. A ladder was leaning against the trap door to the loft.

"I wonder if I can escape that way," said

29

Rupert to himself. Carefully he climbed the
rungs of the ladder until he reached the loft.
But just then he heard the man coming back
and unlocking the door.

Down the ladder Rupert sped and, grabbing
the Professor's machine, hid himself with it
behind a pile of straw in the corner of the shed.

"Where's that bear?" grumbled the man.
"He couldn't have got away . . ."

Then Rupert had a marvellous idea. He
swithed on the machine and twiddled the
knobs so that the sound of his voice would be
carried to the loft.

"I'm up here!" he said, softly.

"Oh, so he's in the loft, is he?" said the thief. He went to the ladder and began to climb up to the loft.

Rupert waited until he was at the top and then quietly tiptoed out of the shed.

"How lucky I am that the man replaced the key in the lock!" he said to himself. "Now I can escape with the Professor's machine all safe and sound!"

When he was safely outside, Rupert turned the key in the lock, using the machine to transfer the sound out of earshot of the thief. Then he ran away as fast as he could.

"I don't know quite where I am," thought Rupert, "But if I keep heading in the same direction I'll come to the end of the wood eventually."

It seemed an awfully long way to the edge of the wood. The machine, which had seemed quite light at first, gradually seemed to become heavier and heavier, until Rupert felt that he would have to stop and put it down. Then he realised that the trees were thinning out.

"Thank goodness! I must be nearly out of the wood!" he gasped. And sure enough, a couple of minutes later he was standing at the edge of the trees, looking across the Common.

"Phew! That was hard work!" he gasped to himself, as he rested against a tree with the voice machine at his feet. And then he saw Constable Growler walking across the Common.

"Hey, Constable Growler!" called Rupert. "Constable Growler! Come over here!"

The policeman looked up and saw Rupert waving to him.

"*Now*, what's the idea, young bear?" he growled, as he came over. "You're not going to tell me any more stories about voices in trees, are you? I've got a lot to do, looking for this escaped thief!"

"I know where he is!" said Rupert, excitedly. "Come on! Follow me!"

"Well, it had better not be another trick of yours," said Constable Growler.

Rupert didn't stop to argue. Careful not to drop the Professor's machine, he led the way back into the wood.

"I'm not too sure of the way," he said, doubtfully. "Do you know a large shed, further into the wood?"

"Why yes, of course I do," said Constable Growler. "A policeman has to know about things like that. Is that where you're taking me?"

"Yes, but if you can lead the way we might get there more quickly," said Rupert. "I've locked the criminal inside, and he won't be able to get out because I've got the key!"

Constable Growler looked very pleased.

"If what you say is true, little bear," he said, "I'll forget all about the way you played that prank on me this morning."

"Oh please, it wasn't a prank, really it wasn't," said Rupert.

"We'll see about that," said Constable Growler, fighting his way through the brambles that lined the path.

Suddenly, they saw the thief ahead of

them. He must have broken out of the hut and was hunting for Rupert.

"Come on," said Constable Growler. "He's going back to the hut." They raced through the wood and hid by the path near the hut.

As the thief approached, Rupert stepped out of the bushes.

"So you tried to trick me, did you!" said the thief angrily. "You'll pay for this!"

"You mean *you'll* pay for this!" said Constable Growler, who had been hiding behind a tree. Taken by surprise, the man had no time to struggle. Before he knew what had happened, he had been handcuffed to the strong arm of Constable Growler and was being led away to the village

"Phew, that was exciting!" thought Rupert. "Just wait until the Professor learns how his machine has helped to catch a thief!"

Then he noticed a sack just inside the shed. Going over to it, he looked inside and found that it was full of pieces of jewellery and other valuable things.

"Hey, wait!" he called to Constable Growler. The policeman stopped and turned to hear what Rupert had to say.

"Here are the things he stole!" shouted Rupert. "Can you come and fetch them be-cause they're too heavy for me to carry!"

Constable Growler and the thief came back to the shed.

"Very well done indeed!" said Constable Growler, picking up the sack. "We'll have no trouble putting this criminal behind bars now that we've found the loot!"

And off he went again, towards Nutwood, with the thief looking very miserable beside him.

"I'd better go back and return the Professor's machine to him at once," thought Rupert. He'll be wondering what has happened to it."

CHAPTER 4

When Rupert arrived back at the Common he was about to go looking for the Professor when he noticed his pals, Willie Mouse and Algy Pug. They were walking across the Common, calling his name.

"They must have been wondering what has happened to me," chuckled Rupert. "I've been gone nearly all afternoon!"

Then he decided that he would play a trick on them. Switching on the machine, he twiddled the knob in the direction of a nearby pond.

"Here I am!" he called. The machine made his voice appear to come from the pond. Algy and Willie ran towards it.

"Rupert must have fallen into the pond!" gasped Willie. "Oh dear!" He crawled on to a

rock at the water's edge to peer into the depths of the pond.

"Whatever shall we do?" breathed Algy, in horror.

Rupert crept up behind them.

"I'm perfectly dry, really!" he said, in a loud voice.

Willie was so surprised at hearing Rupert's voice coming from behind him that he fell into the water!

"Help! Help!" he called. "Mice can't swim!"

So Algy Pug had to dive in and rescue him.

"Lucky it's a hot day, so that we will dry out soon!" laughed Algy. "How did you play that trick, Rupert?"

"I'll tell you later," laughed Rupert. "I didn't mean you to fall in, though. Sorry Willie!"

"What is that machine?" asked Willie, pointing to the voice machine.

"That's the reason I can't tell you much now," said Rupert. "It belongs to the Professor and I've got to get it back to him quickly."

"Oh, we know where he is," said Algy. "He's been looking for you, and we said we'd help him search for you. Come on."

"I've got an idea," said Rupert. "I can play the same trick on the Professor that I played on you just now, and you can see how it works!"

40

They crept into the wood in the direction that Algy said the Professor and his servant had gone. There, before long, they saw the Professor and his faithful servant calling Rupert's name.

"Quick—crouch down behind these bushes," said Rupert. Then, as the friends hid themselves, he switched on the machine again and directed his voice into a tree beside the spot where the Professor was standing.

"Hello, Professor!" came Rupert's voice from the tree.

"Well, would you believe it—Rupert has got stuck up that tree!" said the Professor. Turning to his servant, he said, "I'm too old to climb trees but you could nip up there and see what's the matter with him. Come on, I'll give you a lift up!"

Just as the servant was standing on the Professor's shoulders and holding on to the tree trunk, Rupert skipped up behind them.

"That fooled you, didn't it!" he laughed. The Professor jumped in amazement, and the servant tumbled to the ground in surprise.

"Ouch!" he said. "What a trick to play on us!"

"It's the same one that you played on me!"

laughed Rupert. And then the Professor started to laugh. The servant laughed too, and Willie and Algy joined in. And, as Algy twiddled with the knobs on the machine, their laughter spread from tree to tree, through all the bushes, and all across the Common.

They laughed so hard that everyone came out of their cottages from the other side of the Common to see what all the fun was about. And soon everyone was laughing—everyone, that is, except the thief, who was safely under lock and key!